T HE STORYTELLER pauses at the height of the story. He looks around and takes in all the listening eyes. If he pauses too long, a listener starts a chant and defuses the tension to a manageable emotion.

Ananse stories are unbelievable,
Tell them well, tell them believably!

We breathe, we listen. This time he changes the twist at the end. The story lives and becomes renewed when a storyteller mixes in new spices from his own store.

To my mother, Felicia Twum-Barima,
who told us stories in our childhood. — AB

To my grandmother Sabou Diakité, who said,
"Stories teach us about the importance of all
living creatures."— BWD

NOTE

Most of these stories were told to me as I was grow-
ing up in Ghana. I wrote them as I recollected them,
consulted with other Ghanaians who also remembered the stories, and added my own twists and
details. To clarify details for "Why Pig Has a Short
Snout," I also consulted *Ananse the Spider: Tales from
an Ashanti Village* by Peggy Appiah (Pantheon
Books, 1966). — AB

Groundwood Books / Douglas & McIntyre
720 Bathurst Street, Suite 500
Toronto, Ontario M5S 2R4

Distributed in the USA by Publishers Group West
1700 Fourth Street
Berkeley, CA 94710

We acknowledge the financial support of the Canada
Council for the Arts, the Ontario Arts Council and the
Government of Canada through the Book Publishing
Industry Development Program for our publishing
activities.

National Library of Canada Cataloguing in Publication Data

Badoe, Adwoa
The pot of wisdom: Ananse stories
1st ed.
A Groundwood book.
ISBN 0-88899-429-X
I. Diakité, Baba Wagué. II. Title.
PS8553.A312P67 2001   jC813'.54   C2001-930172-3
PZ7.B32Po 2001

ONTARIO ARTS COUNCIL
CONSEIL DES ARTS DE L'ONTARIO

Baba Wagué Diakité's color illustrations are hand-made
polychromed and glazed earthenware tiles. A bowl by the
artist is shown on page 64. The black-and-white
illustrations are done in marker pen on paper.
Book design by Michael Solomon
Printed and bound in China by Everbest Printing Co. Ltd.

THE POT
OF WISDOM

ANANSE STORIES

ADWOA BADOE

PICTURES BY

BABA WAGUÉ DIAKITÉ

A GROUNDWOOD BOOK
DOUGLAS & McINTYRE
TORONTO VANCOUVER BUFFALO

Why Ananse Lives on the Ceiling

KWEKU ANANSE, the spider, was a farmer and a very good one. He owned the largest farm in town, and he farmed it diligently with his three sons. Early in the morning, even before the cock crowed, they were up and on their way to the farm, where they weeded, watered and tended their crops. They returned home in the evening, exhausted and ready for bed.

Then one year the rains were delayed, and when they came they were scanty. There was a drought in the land, the harvest was poor and food was scarce.

Still Ananse and his sons plodded on, tending their farm as best as they could. Though portions were smaller, they managed to feed the rest of the family and have some left over to sell.

Then a mysterious thing began to happen. Every Monday morning they noticed that someone had been to visit the farm. This was no ordinary visitor. He had apparently sat at his ease, cooked right there on the farm and had himself a feast.

"I would love to catch that thief," the eldest son said.

7

"I bet he thinks he's really smart," added the youngest.

Ananse and his sons planned to keep watch the next Sunday. They waited and waited, but no one turned up. And so it turned out that the nights they watched, the thief stayed away from the farm. But the nights they chose to sleep at home, the thief came to visit.

"It could be the forest dwarves," said Ananse, dropping his voice.

His sons scoffed in disgust.

"It's just a thief who thinks he's smart. If we come up with a very good plan, we'll catch him red-handed," they said.

"Have it your way," Ananse replied. "Count me out of any future watches. These dwarves can get really nasty when they are provoked."

That night the three sons of Ananse hatched a plan. "We can make a small figure like a dwarf to scare off the thief," said the eldest. "Many people are scared of the forest dwarves."

"What if the person is not scared by dwarves?" asked the second.

"I know," exclaimed the third. "We can cover the figure all over with sticky tar, and if the thief touches him he will get caught."

So that Sunday morning, they went off very early to the farm to put their plan in action.

That evening, as was his custom, Ananse put on his Sunday cloth and went to visit with friends.

That evening, as was his custom, the thief went out to enjoy his meal. He saw this tiny dirty figure right where the green plantains grew tall. His first inclination was to turn tail and run. But on second thought he decided to confront the dwarf. No forest dwarf was going to do him out of his dinner.

He had heard that the best way to deal with these dwarves was to threaten them.

"What are you doing here on this farm?" he demanded. When no reply was forthcoming, the thief drew himself up and threatened, "If you do not give me an answer, I shall slap you hard." He shook his fist at the dwarf and waited for a second. Then he struck the tiny figure across the face. "Take that!"

To his astonishment, try as he might, he couldn't free his hand.

"If you do not let go of my hand," he said in frustration, "I'm going to hit you so hard you won't ever forget it." And, *kpao*, he delivered the second blow with such force that he was more stuck than ever.

"Take that and that and let go of me," he said, kicking out at the tiny black creature.

By the time he sensed he had fallen into a trap, his feet and his belly were completely bound to the tar dwarf as though they were Siamese twins. He stuck there in silence waiting for the dawn.

On Monday morning, the three sons of Ananse went to the farm even earlier than usual.

"Won't Father be surprised if our plan worked," they giggled excitedly.

But they were the ones who were in for a shock. For there, stuck on the tar dwarf, was their very own Ananse in his Sunday best. In silence they struggled to free him, ripping apart his cloth in the process. He said not a word but did his best to sneak back home before the town awoke.

Too late for him, some people saw him in his shredded Sunday best.

"Is that not Ananse in hardly any clothes?" They asked one another, gaping openly at him.

"Ananse is naked, Ananse is naked!" chanted the little boys and girls.

"What will we do with a naked Ananse?
Could he be drunk?
Could he be mad?
What could be wrong with a naked Ananse?"

The chant went on and on.

This was too much for his pride, and because the earth wouldn't swallow him up, Ananse did the next best thing and climbed to the farthest corner of his house to hide his face.

From that day onward, spiders have made their homes in the corners of a house.

Ananse
and the Feeding Pot

A S IT happens from time to time, the rains were held up in the sky. The clouds that had gathered soon dispersed, and day after day unrelenting sunshine beat down, shriveling up the young seedlings and baking the earth into hot sand or hard rocky ground.

Soon the people had eaten all the food they had. Many animals died, and those that lived moved in search of water. The crops had failed and now the hunt yielded nothing. This was famine.

In Ananse's village everyone was hungry and weak, or hungry and sick. Day by day they gathered at the chief's courtyard to listen to the elders debate about what could be done to save them. Soon it was clear that there was nothing to be done, and the chief closed court.

That was the day Ananse's son, Ntikuma, disappeared. Ananse put his hands on his head and wept aloud, "Oh, my son, you have probably become meat for some hungry tiger. Will I watch my children die?"

Three days went by, and Ananse decided to hold Ntikuma's

13

funeral. But when the crowds of mourners had gathered, a yellow bird flew overhead and sang a peculiar song.

"Do not mourn for Ntikuma, son of Ananse. He has sent me with great news of dancing, feasting and celebration, so do not mourn for him."

Just as Ananse was deciding what to do, there was a cry among the guests. "There he is, there comes Ntikuma!"

And sure enough there was Ntikuma alive and well, carrying a small pot. A cheer went up. But when he was asked where he had gone and what he had done, he raised his hands and asked for silence.

Then, putting his small pot on the ground, he called out, "Little pot, little pot, prepare a feast that is hot. Prepare a feast for this great lot."

Suddenly there were tables all around, suddenly plates and bowls full of hot steaming food and calabashes full of frothing new palm wine. And without much ado, everyone sat down and ate their fill, and there was even some left for the birds and creatures that lived close by.

Needless to say, Ntikuma became a hero, as day by day his pot made food for all the people of the village.

But after a while, Ananse became quite unhappy. He began to envy Ntikuma and his newfound fame and respect. For now Ntikuma was asked to sit among the counsel of elders, and everyone said what a wise young man he was.

One evening Ananse called Ntikuma. "Tell me, Ntikuma, for people have whispered that you were abducted by strange men. What really happened to you?"

Ntikuma was loath to tell, but Ananse pushed and prodded until at last Ntikuma said, "I will tell you, Father, if you will keep this secret."

"Aha," said Ananse.

"I was particularly hungry that morning when I saw this lizard," said Ntikuma. "I thought, who knows? A lizard may make a tasty morsel."

"Huh," said Ananse, spitting.

"Anyway, I picked up my slingshot and chased the lizard into the woods. Whenever I tried to catch it, it would hide and try to lead me on. It wasn't long before I found that I was lost. I yelled until I felt quite weak and then I lay down under a tall tree, quite sure I would soon die. Then I saw three palm nuts on the ground. I picked up a stone to crack them, to eat the food within. When I hit the first nut, it rolled away and disappeared into a hole. The same thing happened to the next, and then there was only one left. 'Please,' I said, 'do not let this nut roll away.' I picked up the stone and cracked it. The shell flew off, but the tiny hard fruit rolled away and fell down the hole.

"At once I got up and followed the nut down the hole. It seemed to me that I would never hit the ground, but I did. Inside the dark cave sat an old woman. I greeted her in fear, but although she was strange, she was kind, and I served her for two days.

"She sent me to her garden, saying, 'You will find many yams there. Some of them may ask you to uproot them. Leave those alone. But those that protest and say, 'Do not harvest me,' pick those and bring them here.'

"I went into her yam garden and sure enough the loudest voices came from the Pona yams. 'Harvest me,' they called, but I ignored them and harvested instead the thin water yams that protested, 'Leave me alone. Do not harvest me.'"

Ananse thought, "Fool, why harvest water yams when you can have Pona yams?"

"When I took the water yams in, the old woman said, 'Now peel them, throw the fruit away and cook the peel.' I was surprised, but I did as she said and soon the water was boiling. When I eventually strained away the water, there was the most delicious yam, which we ate with palava sauce.

"Then the old woman said, 'Son, you have been faithful. Go into the next room and pick a pot. There are many pots in that room. Several of them will call to you to pick them, but do not! Whichever begs to be left alone, pick that one and be on your way. My yellow bird will tell you what to do.'"

"Aha," said Ananse, eager to hear the rest.

"That is exactly what happened. In the room were a hundred, maybe a thousand pots. Huge ones, small ones, gold, silver, brass and earthenware pots. But the ones I really liked all said, 'Pick me, please,' and the only one that said, 'Leave me alone,' was this small pot. I picked it up, thanked the old lady and left, her bird leading the way."

"Ho," said Ananse. "You should have chosen a big pot. How much more it would have done."

But Ntikuma said, "Who knows? Better to take instruction from the owner."

"Humph," said Ananse. "Trust me on this. You should have chosen the largest."

Ananse did not sleep that night. All he could think about was pots and more pots.

"I must try to get a better pot," he thought. "Tomorrow… tomorrow."

The next day, although the whole village was well fed, Ananse pretended to chase a lizard and went off into the woods as Ntikuma had described. Seeing the tall tree, he lay down.

Lo! There were three nuts and a stone. He cracked the first nut and out came the fruit. Looking around, Ananse nudged the fruit until it rolled into a nearby hole. He cracked the second nut which also stayed quite still until a determined Ananse poked the nut down the hole.

Poking the third nut into the hole, Ananse himself jumped in and there was the old woman.

"Grandmother," said Ananse (when it was clear the old woman was saying nothing), "would you like me to cook you a yam?"

"If you wish," she replied. "When you get to the garden, leave the yams alone that call out to you to harvest them. Instead take the yams that ask to be left alone."

"Yes, Grandmother," said Ananse.

Outside, the huge Pona yam called out, "Harvest me!" and the skinny water yams called out, "Don't take me, don't take me!"

Ananse considered for a while. Any child knew that the huge Pona yams would taste better. So he brought in some Pona yams.

The old woman sat on her stool and took no notice, except to say, "When you peel them, throw the fruit away and cook the peel."

"Crazy old woman," thought Ananse. And of course he threw the peels away and cooked the fruit.

After the yams had boiled a long while, Ananse strained off the water, but there was nothing but gravel in the pot.

At last a rather hungry Ananse said, "Grandmother, will you not give me a pot to take away?"

"Go into that room," she said. "The pots will call out to you, but take only the one that says, 'Leave me alone.'"

Ananse forgot about his hunger. This was the reason he had journeyed deep into the forest.

He opened the door, and in a tall narrow room were all the pots. Gold, silver, brass, bronze, copper, terra cotta, earthenware, glazed, fired, smoked and painted. And they all called out to Ananse.

One said, "I will cook you exotic dishes."

Another said, "I will smoke you the best meat."

"You will never go hungry if you choose me," said yet another.

Only one small pot begged, "Don't take me, leave me alone!" That pot was even smaller than Ntikuma's.

"Of course I won't take you," thought Ananse, reaching for the huge golden pot that promised feasts as well as money.

Ananse shut the door and thanked the old lady. "Grandmother, I will take my leave now, if I may." The old lady took no notice as Ananse found his way out with the help of the yellow bird.

"Yellow bird," said Ananse. "Fly to my people and ask them to call a celebration, for I will return home in triumph. I have descended into the underworld and returned rich. Let them meet in my honor."

The people gathered to wait for Ananse. The drummers started their drumming, the singers started singing and the dancers stomped and stamped their way through the victory dance until Ananse arrived.

"Here, my people, is the golden pot. It will prepare food such as you have never seen in your life. Golden pot, I command a feast."

There was a deep rumble in the huge pot, then a swishing and swirling, then a frothing and bubbling. Out of the pot crawled bugs and beetles, caterpillars and lizards, snakes and worms. Plate upon plate full of gruesome creepy crawlies.

Above, the yellow bird's laughter could be heard, much like the voice of the old lady.

"Eat your greed, Ananse. Eat your jealousy and your envy. You could have asked for rain or animals for the hunt. Now eat your disobedience!!"

The people looked everywhere for Ananse to punish him for dishonoring them, but Ananse had climbed up to the corner of the ceiling to hide his shame in his web.

Ananse Becomes
the Owner of Stories

ONLY ONE thing concerned Ananse—how he would be remembered when he died! It was good for one to leave behind a monument. It was good to be remembered among the great and to be sung as one of the heroes.

But Ananse had no military prowess, no awesome strength, no wise proverbs. Only his wits. He lived by his wits.

"It would be nice," he thought, "if all stories belonged to me."

"Ananse stories," he said aloud. He thought it sounded good. Then everyone would remember him when they passed the evenings telling stories.

He lost no time passing the title around. But when the king of the forest lands heard of it, he said to Ananse, "Great names are given to those who do great things. What have you done to deserve such honor?"

"Try me, great king, and you will find that I deserve no less," replied Ananse, undaunted.

"As yet no one has captured alive these three. Wowa, the entire household of honeybees, Aboatia of the forest dwarves and Nanka the python. Do that and the ownership of stories is yours."

"I am at your service, Great One," Ananse replied. "For although I am small, I have learned the weaknesses of the great. In three days you shall have proof of my greatness."

Ananse spent the night planning his conquests, and early the next morning he was on his way.

Everyone knows how busy honeybees are and how ill-tempered they become when they are disturbed and how they sting when you make them mad. Ananse bore this in mind when he ventured to their hive.

"What a great number of you must live in here," he said by way of greeting.

"Three hundred of us," replied the head worker.

"What?" shouted Ananse. "Did you say two hundred?"

"Three hundred," said the head worker again.

"Oh. Someone else said two hundred just last week," said Ananse. "There must be two hundred of you."

"Three hundred," buzzed the irritated head worker.

"Two hundred," said Ananse defiantly. Before long, many bees joined in the argument and everyone was calling out the numbers they had counted.

"Okay," shouted Ananse above the buzz. "To settle this once and for all, why don't I count you?"

The suggestion seemed fair to all concerned. Ananse produced a bottle and said, "You simply have to fly one at a time into this bottle and I shall count as you go in."

First to go in was the head worker, and one by one they all went in, even the queen bee.

"And how many are we?" asked the bees.

"Three hundred," said Ananse, sealing the bottle.

"I told you so," said the head worker.

22

"Yes, but I have you all now!" said Ananse. And although they buzzed with all their might, Ananse carried them off to his home.

The next day Ananse cut a huge hand of golden ripe bananas from his farm and tugged it to a part of the forest where the dwarf people lived. Now, the dwarf people were very smart. They could run swiftly and silently through the forest at such speeds that a man's eye could not see them. One could only feel the wind. They could also stand so still that people passed them off as old tree stumps. Indeed, only a few people had actually seen a forest dwarf, and most people believed they did not exist.

Pausing in the deep forest, Ananse announced as though he was speaking to himself, "I am so exhausted. I'm simply going to leave my bananas here and return for them tomorrow." He then pretended to leave, but instead hid under a plantain tree and covered himself with its broad leaves.

It was not long before a forest dwarf crawled out of his hiding place.

"Oh, ripe golden bananas I love best! I had better eat my fill before he returns." The dwarf ate until he could hardly stand. Then he ate until he could hardly sit. And still he ate until he lay on his back and rolled about with a belly ache.

Out came Ananse. The dwarf tried to run away, but he slipped on the banana skins and fell flat on his tummy. Ananse caught him by the scruff of his neck and dropped him into his sack and carried him away to his home.

The next day Ananse was walking by the river where Nanka the python bathed. "Oh, Nanka, everyone talks about your magnificent skin and your majestic length."

"Oh, yes," Nanka agreed. "There is none as magnificent as I."

"I wonder myself exactly how tall you are, because I cut this

23

bamboo branch on my farm and it seems to me it is longer than you."

"Nonsense," hissed the python.

"Well, if you don't mind, could you lie down beside it for a minute, just to prove me wrong?"

"All right," said the python. "But be quick." After a minute the python asked, "So, what do you think now, Ananse? Which of us is longer?"

"Mmmm," Ananse pondered aloud. "It's hard to say because your neck and tail keep moving. Hang on and I'll just tie the bamboo to you for only a second, just to keep you still."

Ananse quickly tied the python's neck and tail securely to the bamboo branch.

"There we are," he said. "I've got you, sir!"

And with that he carried the python, the honeybees and the forest dwarf to the king of the forest lands.

The king was impressed. He acknowledged Ananse's greatness and made him the owner of stories.

Even today, everywhere stories are told, the name of Ananse is mentioned as the owner of the best stories.

Ananse
the Even-handed Judge

ANANSE'S FAME had spread afar as a result of his past deeds, and many people now recognized him as a man of much wisdom. As a result the great king of the forest lands appointed him to be the judge of two villages. It was a job that Ananse took seriously. Day after day he held court in one of the villages and judged wisely for all the people. He became well known for his even-handed judgments.

One Thursday, he received messengers from one of the nearby villages, who invited him to attend a marriage ceremony as a guest of high honor on Saturday. Ananse was pleased to accept.

The messengers had barely left when another group of messengers from the chief of the other village requested the presence of Ananse at the funeral of the chief's aunt on the same day.

"This poses a slight problem," said Ananse. "You see, I have already given my word that I would attend a marriage ceremony at the other village."

"Do you mean you have declined to attend the funeral of the chief's aunt, in preference to a marriage ceremony?" asked the messenger. "Now that poses a real problem with our chief whom you have slighted!"

"I beg your pardon," said Ananse. "I shall be there. Tell Nana it will be an honor to mourn with him." The messengers left at once.

Now Ananse pondered what to do. As a great judge, his word was his bond, and he knew no way to excuse himself from one or the other engagement. He had to find a way to defer to both parties and maintain his impartiality.

Eventually a plan came to him. He would send one of his sons to each village ahead of time. Each son would take along a very strong rope spun of spider silk, which Ananse had tied around his waist. (Remember that Ananse was still a spider and good at spinning webs.) When it came time for a party to start, all his son had to do was tug his rope hard. Ananse would go to the place toward which he was tugged first. Then at the first opportunity he would leave for the next village. (In those days there was no accurate way of telling time. People would say quite broadly, sun up or sun down.)

On the Saturday of the festivities, Ananse bathed and dressed himself in his best clothes—dark enough for mourning and bright enough for rejoicing. He secured the silken ropes firmly around his waist and sent his sons on their way. Then he sat down to wait, quite pleased with himself.

Eventually he felt a tug toward his left side. "The marriage ceremony has started," he thought. "I had better be on my way." No sooner had he started off when the rope on his right side was pulled hard. And then both ropes were pulling so hard that Ananse could hardly breathe.

The wise judge had forgotten to tell his sons to stop pulling after the initial tug, and now the brothers were involved in a tug of Ananse, which nearly tore him clean in two.

28

By the time passersby freed Ananse from his ropes, he could hardly walk. He was quite unable to go to either of the ceremonies, and his great reputation for wisdom was ruined as the people laughed at his folly. Fearing that no one would ever listen to his judgments again, he fled to the corner of his room to hide his face.

Ananse
the Forgetful Guest

ANANSE HAD journeyed for miles and miles to take a message from the king of the forest lands to the king of the coast lands. Now after several days of tracking through the forest, his journey was almost at an end. Ananse could think only of one thing—food.

On the nights he had spent in the forest, he had dreamed of food—hot steaming rice and spinach sauces, or soft balls of fufu with crab and palm nut soup. He had awakened twice with saliva drooling and nothing to eat except for some moist leaves and a few bugs or bush rats when he could catch them.

Now he was at last in the great town of Po-Ano, a guest of none other than the king of the coast lands. He would deliver his message. Then, as tradition demanded, he would bathe and eat.

The king was a kind man, and after making sure that Ananse had been given a room, water to bathe and a change of clothes, he instructed his senior wife to prepare a meal for him.

Imagine the pleasure Ananse felt as the smell of cooking food filled his nostrils.

"Let me guess," he chuckled to himself. "This will be rice and chicken stew that's cooking." Unable to wait any longer, Ananse dressed quickly and followed his nose to the kitchen.

"Ah, Mr. Ananse, you are most welcome," said the king's wife. "You must be very hungry after your long journey."

"Yes, indeed," replied Ananse. "Right now, with the smell of your food filling this room, it is my pleasure to be hungry."

With a flourish, the king's wife lifted the lid off Ananse's bowl. But at the sight of the food, Ananse collapsed, for in the bowl was the most despised of foods—dried cassava mash. In the forest lands it was called Face-the-Wall, because you never wanted people to know that you were so poor that you had to eat that food. Certainly it was not the food to serve a guest.

Ananse was too shocked to even appreciate the delicious chicken soup the king's wife had cooked to go with the dried cassava mash.

"Help, help," cried the king's wife. "Our guest has taken ill." By the time help arrived, Ananse had emerged from his sudden faint.

"It is nothing, madam," said Ananse weakly. "Only a small hereditary malady, for cassava is forbidden to me. Even the sight of it affects me."

"Oh, dear," said the king's wife. "I am afraid this is going to be a difficult visit for you. In this town we eat cassava at every meal."

Impossible, thought Ananse. This must be a trick to test my resolve. Why would people eat cassava at every meal?

But they did! In the mornings they ate cassava porridge, in the afternoons they ate cassava mash, and in the evenings they ate their cassava roasted.

Ananse had to go out each day to find moist leaves and bugs to eat, for the news had spread that cassava was forbidden to him.

The last day of Ananse's visit fell on the harvest celebrations. A great feast was anticipated. By now Ananse wished fervently that he could be allowed just a small bite of cassava, which the people of Po-Ano cooked in a myriad of delightful ways. There were spicy cassava fries, cassava and vegetable stir-fry, not to mention the soups and stews with which cassava was served.

That night, he hatched a plan.

The next day dawned bright, as though even the skies knew of the harvest festival and the feasting that would soon take place. Everywhere people bustled about preparing food and preparing themselves for the feast in the public square where the king would be in attendance. The royal dais was erected, and seating was arranged around a central clearing where speeches and prayers were to be said.

Early that afternoon the people of Po-Ano gathered for the festivities adorned in brightly colored cloths of rich design. Ceremonial silk and two-piece suits sewn in traditional fashion were enhanced by jewelry made of gold, silver, beads and polished wood.

Finally the king made his entrance. But Ananse was nowhere to be found. The prayers were said and the speeches made. Gift bearers brought firewood and other gifts to the king.

Then in the lull before the dancing started, a very odd figure in the rough garb of a farm laborer appeared holding a machete—a misfit among the crowd of well-dressed harvest-time jubilators.

"Ananse!" the king thundered from his dais. "What is the meaning of this…this insult!"

"I beg your pardon, sir, but I thought we were going harvesting today," said Ananse.

"No!" shouted the crowd. "Today is the harvest celebration!"

"Oh, no," said Ananse, hanging his head in apparent shame. "You must think I'm crazy but really I'm not. It is just this awful forgetfulness that comes over me occasionally. It is the same forgetfulness that made me say cassava was forbidden to me when actually it is one of my favorite vegetables!"

The king was pleased to forgive him and pleased that he did eat cassava. The people of Po-Ano were pleased to share their feast with him. Many secretly thought that Ananse was kind of strange, but since his visit people sometimes plead his kind of forgetfulness whenever they are caught in a sticky situation.

The Mat Confidences

Abena Nkoroma was the ninth child of the great king of the forest lands. She was a beautiful young woman, and many men desired to marry her. Day in and day out young men from far and near came to pledge their love. Some sang for her, others danced and many wrestled. Some hunted wild animals and showed her their vast lands and wealth. But Abena would have none of them.

Then one day the great king threw a challenge to all the men. The town criers beat their gong-gongs, announcing that if anyone could rid an acre of the king's land of nettles and thorns without scratching or complaining, that man could have Abena in marriage.

Believing that no one could weed an acre of land overgrown with nettles and thorns without scratching, Abena Nkoroma peeked through her window and laughed at all who tried.

The older men thought no woman was worth the trouble, but the younger men would often try. One and all failed because the nettles were itchy and the thorns prickly. It was hard not to stop and scratch and harder still not to say, "*Aiee!*"

One Wednesday morning, a market day, Ananse decided to try.

"Of course she's worth it," he said to an older man. "She's the king's daughter, she's the most beautiful woman and marrying her will make me royalty." So, shaking off his cloth, as men do when there is work to do, he picked up his machete and sliced through rows and rows of nettles and thorns.

Before long a large group of market-goers stopped by to watch. As he worked he sang a song.

"Abena Nkoroma, Abena Nkoroma,
There is a man to see you, Abena Nkoroma.
Ask him what he wants of me?
Abena Nkoroma, he's in love with you.
Is he a warrior, is he a prince?
Is he someone deserving my love?
Abena Nkoroma, he's a weary man.
Tell him NO, tell him to GO!"

It was such a provocative song that soon everyone was singing, and Ananse, encouraged by the chant, worked hard.

But the nettles stung and the thorns pricked, and soon Ananse punctuated his song with bursts of *"Aiee!"* as though it were part of the song. And the crowd happily sang with him. The nettles and the thorns stung and pricked more, and Ananse changed his song.

"Ask me why I am in love with her."

Immediately the crowd screamed, "Ananse, why, O, why?"

"Haven't you heard of Abena Nkoroma?
Her arms, they say, are slender and supple,
And when she dances she moves this way and that.
Her legs, they say, are long and smooth,

And when she dances she moves this way and that.
Her neck, they say, is as the tower,
Her eyes like the moon in a cloudless sky.
Her nose sits straight like a linguist's staff,
And her lips are as sweet as fresh palm wine."

Whenever he mentioned a body part, Ananse would pause to rub and scratch himself, pretending all the while that he was merely describing Abena. And in this way and with the crowd's participation, Ananse weeded the acre of land without obviously scratching or whining.

The report was made to the king that Ananse had been successful in weeding the acre of land without scratching or crying out. So he handed over Abena Nkoroma, and they became man and wife.

A few days later, as Abena and her husband Ananse lay on their sleeping mats, Abena asked Ananse, "However did you manage to weed my father's land without scratching?"

"Ho!" said Ananse, eager to impress Abena. And he explained to her how he had chosen a market day for the support of the crowd, and the songs and gestures he had used to complete the task, while not obviously scratching or showing his pain.

"Ho!" said Abena in triumph. "This time I have got you."

"What does that mean?" asked Ananse, bewildered, for he had expected praise for his craftiness. Instead Abena rolled over onto her side and chuckled. "I shall tell my father the king of this matter. How hot is the water you have fallen in, Ananse."

"Abena, my wife," Ananse pleaded. "Please do not expose me, your husband. It is not right to tell confidences shared between a man and his wife. Not sleeping-mat confidences!"

But Abena was decided and, turning her back on Ananse, she fell into a deep sleep. Ananse, however, tossed and turned until his crafty mind discovered a way out.

Deep in the night, Ananse called Abena's name three times. When she did not respond, he carefully fetched a small pail of water and poured it on her sleeping mat. Then he went back to sleep on his own side.

At dawn he woke up and, with a cry of outrage, he woke up Abena.

"Ho, Abena! What is this I see? The woman I worked so hard to marry wet our mat at night. Shame, for I have married a bed wetter. I must tell the counsel of elders, for I have been cheated."

It was Abena Nkoroma's turn to plead and beg, but Ananse would hear none of it.

Eventually Abena said, "My husband, let us consider this incident a mat confidence."

"Well," said Ananse triumphantly, "if you agree to keep the other matter a mat confidence!"

And so Ananse preserved his life and his marriage, as people preserve their marriages to this day by keeping mat confidences private.

Ananse
and the Pot of Wisdom

ANANSE IS a very special spider, well known for his wit and wisdom. He lives like other spiders, in corners and on ceilings. The tricky thing about him is that he looks no different from other spiders. In fact, he may be the very next spider who comes your way.

Everybody knew that Ananse was wise, for he boasted loud and clear. In his high-pitched voice he laughed at fools and spoke louder than everyone else.

One very sunny day, Sky God called Ananse up to the skies to have a chat.

"Without a doubt," Ananse said, "of all the animals you created, there is none as wise as I."

Sky God said in a quiet voice, "Could you do some work for me? Go about the earth and collect all wisdom for me. When you have brought it up to me, I will name you the Sage of All Time."

Ananse hid a smile. "That's easy, sir," he said. "I will be back in three days with the wisdom of the world."

Now, Ananse, as selfish as he was, had already traveled the length and breadth of the earth and collected every shred of wisdom. He kept it all in a giant pot in his secret hiding place.

He slid down to his home on a fine woven thread. He took a rest in the shade and had a lazy day.

The next day he started out to take the pot full of wisdom to Sky God way up in the skies.

It was a huge pot and very heavy. As Ananse tugged it behind him, he was more than filled with pride. When others asked to help, he would say in a stand-offish way, "This work is top secret for a very high official."

To get up to the skies where Sky God lived, you had to climb a tall coconut tree that grew beyond the clouds right up into the heavens. Ananse stopped to consider the best way to carry his load. He could not carry it on his head because he needed all his eight arms to creep up the tree. In the end he strapped the pot tightly to his back and made his way slowly up the tree.

From afar everyone saw his clumsy figure scaling up so slowly. They knew he was going to meet with Sky God himself. The people gathered under the tree to watch him make his way. And all the while they wondered what he had in the giant pot.

Inch by inch Ananse climbed. He was looking forward to the fame his great feat deserved. Meanwhile the sun moved slowly across the wide sky.

Just before the sun set, he paused and carefully wove a web to keep himself secure.

He could hardly sleep at all that night. He was so excited!

At daybreak Ananse woke up and continued his climb. A greater crowd was gathered below, waving and cheering him on. He pressed on, never mind his aching muscles. He had an appointment in heaven, and he was going to make it there.

46

Higher and higher Ananse kept up the pace, until the light of the moon reminded him to take a rest.

That night he dreamt he wore a crown given to him by Sky God himself. On it was written "The Sage of All Time."

Another day passed and a very tired Ananse was near the end of his journey. Below, the crowd let out a cheer.

It was a great moment for Ananse and, as pride filled his chest, he raised all his arms in a victory wave.

It was a shocking moment when he plummeted down to earth. He hit the ground with a bang and the pot broke in a million pieces. Wisdom scattered left and right, to the very ends of the earth.

Ananse lay there in a heap, sobbing his heart out. What he had worked so hard to collect was now out of his grasp. Now everyone and every fool had a little bit of wisdom. He could not claim that all wisdom was his alone.

Then Sky God whispered in his ear, "I gave you eight arms, Ananse. If you really had all wisdom, you would not have waved them all."

Ananse and the Singing Cloak

ONE YEAR a strange thing happened. The rains rained only on Chameleon's farm and not at all on Ananse's farm. Ananse watched in dismay as his crops shriveled up and died while Chameleon's plants grew tall and bore much fruit. In vain he tried to go into partnership with Chameleon but, being no fool, Chameleon declined.

Soon Ananse set his crafty mind to finding a way to swindle Chameleon out of his produce.

Everyone knows that Chameleon makes no paths, preferring to walk over grass and leaves to get where he is going. Taking this into account, Ananse told his children to make a path from their hut to Chameleon's farm by walking to and fro throughout the night. They did this for several weeks until an obvious foot path was made. Now Ananse was ready for his devious trick.

One day after Chameleon had skittered over leaves and grass to get to his farm, he was surprised to find Ananse and his sons harvesting his crops.

"Stop this at once," he shouted. "What are you doing on my farm?"

51

"Your farm?" asked Ananse. "You must be sleep talking. Everyone knows this is my farm." They argued for hours and very nearly fought, but eventually Chameleon took the matter to the chief to settle.

The chief was greatly puzzled by the unusual complaint. However, taking into account Ananse's reputation as a great farmer and the proof of a well-trodden path from Ananse's hut to the disputed farm, he gave the farm to Ananse, who triumphantly harvested another man's crop.

Chameleon was very sore about the loss of his farm and spent a whole month brooding and planning how to get his revenge. Eventually he got up and, putting on his most ragged clothes, went to beg Ananse to allow him to glean the remains of the crops. This Ananse allowed, seeing that Chameleon was suitably humbled and willing to make peace.

As there was hardly anything left on the farm, Chameleon returned only with dried vines of yam. Then he made a deep hollow in the ground with a very narrow opening.

After this he spent the days quietly, catching flies and making himself a most interesting cloak of dried yam vines and buzzing flies.

And so it was that at the harvest festival of yams, Chameleon wore his great coat, walking majestically while it swayed and buzzed all around him. It soon became known as the singing cloak. At the festival, Ananse was named the best farmer on account of the size of his yams, but all the talk was about Chameleon's cloak. And Ananse yearned for the cloak.

After the festival, Ananse went over to Chameleon's house to offer to buy the cloak.

"Oh, no," Chameleon said. "It is much too special to sell."

Eventually he agreed to exchange the cloak for enough food to fill his hole. Ananse, taking a peek at the deceptively small opening, wholeheartedly agreed.

"I'll give you twice the food it takes to fill your hole," he said.

It took Ananse a week and a half as well as all his food to fill Chameleon's hole. Chameleon, who was quite reasonable by nature, freed Ananse from the rest of his debt and generously gave him the singing cloak as well.

But when Ananse tried it on, the dried vines that held the buzzing flies had rotted through. When a gust of wind blew, the vines fell away and the flies escaped, leaving Ananse with a cloak of shredded, half-rotten yam vines that barely covered him at all. The little children laughed and pointed fingers at the half-clothed Ananse, who skittered up the nearest tree and hid in a web he had made.

Chameleon laughed fit to kill himself. But, knowing Ananse's cunning, he is always on the lookout and keeps changing his color just to hide from Ananse.

Why Pig Has a Short Snout

IT USED TO be, not so very long ago, that the pig had a trunk as long as the elephant's. And so proud was he of his great trunk! With it he could suck up water for his very own shower, and he could water the plants in his herb garden. He could snort and blow a scary tune, and he could curl his trunk around and tie it in knots.

In those days, Pig was also a money lender. His success was due to the fact that no one ever made off with his money. With his trunk he would sniff and find the culprit and drag him from his hiding place. Pig was very proud of his useful trunk.

Now, Ananse borrowed some money from Pig to pay the dowry for his son's marriage. And because Ananse liked to keep up appearances, he had borrowed a lot to show his worth.

A month passed by, and it was time to pay back Pig. But Ananse, it seemed, had forgotten his debt.

"Here I come," said Pig, "with my long trunk to seek and find."

But when he got to Ananse's house, Ananse pleaded for another week. "By then my debtors will have paid me back, and I'll be ready when you come by."

"You had better have my money," threatened Pig. "Or else you shall have the thrashing of your life." Then he waved his trunk in the air and went off to collect from someone else.

The next week Pig returned, snorting and blowing his impatience.

"My money, Ananse. I want my money!"

"Now you have startled me," said Ananse, looking down a long bamboo pole. "See, I have dropped your money down my bamboo pole. Now I have to think how to get it out!"

"I'll get it," said a mollified Pig. "It was my fault. I'll reach in with my trunk to get it out." And so Pig reached deep into the hollow bamboo pole.

"I can't find it," he said.

"Reach a little deeper," said Ananse. "You need to stretch just a little farther." So Pig strained and pushed.

When he realized his trunk could go no farther, he tried to pull it out. But he couldn't. He was stuck. He moved his head this way and that, but he was stuck. He wiggled and rolled and banged his head, but he was stuck.

"Help," he cried. "Help, help!" But Ananse had gone to hide in his web, and none of the other creatures was willing to help.

Finally, with one big shake of Pig's head, the bamboo pole fell off, alas with his trunk. And it never grew back.

As for Ananse, he did not pay his debt, and Pig never bothered him again.

Ananse
and the Birds

ONE EVENING, just as the sun set, Ananse gathered his children around the fire and told them stories about his exploits. As the night wore on, his tales became taller and taller, as he liberally sprinkled them with pepper and salt.

At last, unable to stand it any longer, his wife exclaimed, "It is a wonder that you have not as yet flown with the birds."

Ananse replied, "Ah, that I have not yet done. However, if the birds can do it and even the lowly housefly, then I, Ananse, no doubt can also fly." And with that he bid his children goodnight and retired to plan his next adventure.

For the next few days Ananse was unusually nice to the sparrows and the crows that flew about. He was even nice to the chickens and ducks that scratched for food. He would hand them a morsel and chat with them. He never asked a thing of them—except a feather here and a feather there. And then he stuck the feathers together with rubber and tar to fashion a pair of wings.

For the next week he practiced flying at night when no one was watching, except an old owl who hunted by night.

"Ananse," she hooted, "*whoo-oo*. The skies are for birds, *oo-oo*. It takes more than wings to be a creature of the skies, *oo-oo*."

"Shut up, you old bat," retorted Ananse. "Go to bed if there is nothing to hunt!" And he went on practicing and making adjustments to his wings.

One day, as the birds were preparing for flight, Ananse approached them and asked if he could come along.

"Why, of course," said Crow. "If you can fly, you may attend the feast of the birds on the mountain far away." Then he and all the birds started crowing aloud, amused at Ananse's request.

Imagine their surprise when Ananse produced his wings and started to fly.

"First a hop on my right front leg. Then a jump and a skip and I'm up." And there was Ananse flying with the best of the lot.

Now the birds were not very happy about that, but Crow had spoken and he had to keep his word. Up they flew, higher and higher above the clouds. Up where the air was thinner and flying was much harder, and still Ananse kept up with the birds. Then at last they were on the mountain where all the birds were ready to feast.

Ananse could not believe his eyes. So partial was he to delicious food that he ate and ate, forgetting entirely that he was a guest. He shoved and quarreled with all the birds about meat and bones and leaves and yams and made a nuisance of himself. Soon he was so full that he fell asleep.

One by one, each bird took away the feathers they had given him. And while he was still asleep, they stole away in the silence of the evening, leaving Crow, who prodded Ananse awake.

"See you down below, friend Ananse," said Crow.

"Oh, please," said Ananse, when he realized he had hardly any feathers left. "Could you help me to get down?"

"Of course," said Crow, pretending not to understand. And with that he pushed Ananse off the mountain.

"*Eeeeeeeee!*" screamed Ananse as he hurtled through the sky at top speed.

"*Whooooo,*" came an eerie sound from the darkening skies. "The skies are for birds, I told you so. It takes more than wings to be a creature of the skies," sang the owl who was out hunting.

"Help," screamed Ananse. "*Eeeeeeee.*"

"Press on your belly," urged the owl. From out of Ananse's belly came fine silk from all the food he had eaten at the feast of the birds. And the owl, taking hold of the threads, hung them securely on a branch of a tree, breaking Ananse's fall to certain doom.

As he hung from the branch of the tree, Ananse wisely considered the owl's advice.

"No more flying for me," he said. Instead he learned to spin fancy webs so that he would never fall again.